Mary Jane carried the ~~cat upstairs to her~~
mother's bedroom and tied the ribbon in
a bow around the cat's neck. "Just see
yourself, cat." Mary Jane put her on the
dressing table in front of the mirror.

The cat looked at herself with pride.
"The witch would hardly know me."

"Tell me about the witch," begged
Mary Jane. "What was she doing here?"

"It's Wednesday, and she's a Wednesday
Witch."

"What's a Wednesday Witch?"

"Her magic is at its best on Wednesday.
The rest of the week she works on her
spells. On Wednesday she comes out of
her cave and looks for mischief. She said
she smelled mischief on your street today."

RUTH CHEW

THE WEDNESDAY WITCH

with illustrations by the author

A STEPPING STONE BOOK™

Random House New York

To Helen,
who asked for
a witch story

Visit us on the Web!
SteppingStonesBooks.com
randomhousekids.com

Educators and librarians, for a variety of teaching tools,
visit us at RHTeachersLibrarians.com

Library of Congress Cataloging-in-Publication Data
Chew, Ruth, author, illustrator.
The Wednesday witch / by Ruth Chew ; with illustrations by the author.—
First Random House edition.
p. cm
"A Stepping Stone Book."
Originally published: New York : Scholastic, Inc., 1969.
Summary: The arrival of a witch who travels by magic vacuum cleaner is
only the beginning of Mary Jane's strange adventures.
ISBN 978-0-449-81556-4 (trade pbk.) — ISBN 978-0-449-81558-8 (ebook)
[1. Witches—Fiction. 2. Cats—Fiction.] I. Title.
PZ7.C429We 2015 [Fic]—dc23 2014032383

Printed in the United States of America
10 9 8 7 6 5 4 3 2 1

This book has been officially leveled by using the F&P Text Level Gradient™
Leveling System.

THE
WEDNESDAY
WITCH

MISCHIEF

"Now don't let any stranger into the house, Mary Jane," said Mrs. Brooks. "I'm going to the supermarket. If the doorbell rings, look through the peep hole first to see who is there. If it's someone you don't know, don't open the door. And don't get into mischief while I'm gone."

Mary Jane watched her mother walk down the tree-lined Brooklyn street. As soon as Mrs. Brooks turned the corner, Mary Jane ran upstairs.

Today she would have plenty of time to go through all the things on her mother's dressing table. Mary Jane wouldn't dare touch them when her mother was around. But now she could even pick them up and try them out.

There were so many things—tiny nail scissors, jars of face cream, a pink satin ribbon, three lipsticks, a big box of bath powder, an eyebrow pencil, a magnifying mirror, and—right in the middle, sparkling like a big jewel—a new bottle of perfume. It was called "Mischief."

Mary Jane twisted the stopper and slowly pulled it out of the bottle. At once the room was filled with a strange, exciting smell.

The doorbell rang. Mary Jane ran downstairs, and was about to open the door. Then she remembered what her mother had said. "Before you open the door, look through the peep hole." But the peep hole was high up on the door. So she went to get a dining room chair to stand on. The doorbell rang again.

Mary Jane was pushing the chair against the door when the brass door knocker banged loudly. Whoever was outside must be very impatient, Mary Jane thought. She climbed up on the chair. The door knocker banged again.

A harsh voice screamed, "Is anybody home?"

Mary Jane put one eye to the peep hole and looked out. On the doorstep stood a short fat woman wearing a tall pointed hat. She had a vacuum cleaner with her, the kind that looks like a large jug. A skinny black cat with big yellow eyes and a ragged tail sat on top of the vacuum cleaner. And the hose to the vacuum cleaner was coiled around the fat woman's neck like a big snake.

Mary Jane tried to make her voice sound deep and growly. "Who are you?"

"I want to show you a vacuum cleaner," said the woman. She seemed to be trying to make her voice low and sweet, but it sounded like a scratchy whisper. "It's a lovely vacuum cleaner. I will clean your house for you."

She looked so funny standing there in her long black dress and her pointy hat that Mary Jane could not help teasing. "You can't fool me," she said in the same deep voice. "You are a wicked witch! Go away!"

With a loud click Mary Jane shut the peep hole. Then, ever so quietly, she opened it again and looked out. She saw the short fat woman shake her fist, stamp her foot, and then sit down on the vacuum cleaner. The woman held the metal wand in front of her and shouted, "Home, James!"

The vacuum cleaner rose into the air with the witch. Mary Jane jumped off the chair and opened the door. She saw the witch sail higher and higher, over the tree-tops, higher than the apartment building on the corner. Mary Jane watched until the witch sailed away out of sight.

"Meow." It was the thin black cat, sitting sadly on the doorstep.

The witch must have forgotten her cat, thought Mary Jane, or perhaps she is trying to trick me.

"Meow," said the cat again. Then, to Mary Jane's surprise, it said, "I'm hungry."

Mary Jane couldn't help feeling sorry for the skinny cat. "There's some tuna fish left over from lunch," she said. "Would you like that?"

"I don't know," said the cat. "I've never had fish. All the witch feeds me is toads—when she remembers to feed me at all. And she has a pot of witch's brew that she thinks is delicious, but I can't stand it."

"What's your name, cat?"

"The witch calls me 'Hey, you!'"

"Oh, you poor thing!" cried Mary Jane, and she scooped up the cat. It was so light! Mary Jane could feel all the bones under the scraggly fur. She carried the cat into the house and shut the door.

Mary Jane fed the cat in the kitchen. The cat ate the tuna fish hungrily but daintily. Then she drank a bowl full of milk. When she had finished she washed her face, smoothed her whiskers, and licked herself all over.

Soon the black fur was smooth and shining.

"You need a ribbon! There is a pink satin one that came on Mother's perfume."

Mary Jane carried the cat upstairs to her mother's bedroom and tied the ribbon in a bow around the cat's neck. "Just see yourself, cat." Mary Jane put her on the dressing table in front of the mirror.

The cat looked at herself with pride. "The witch would hardly know me."

"Tell me about the witch," begged Mary Jane. "What was she doing here?"

"It's Wednesday, and she's a Wednesday Witch."

"What's a Wednesday Witch?"

"Her magic is at its best on Wednesday. The rest of the week she works on her spells. On Wednesday she comes out of her cave and looks for mischief. She said she smelled mischief on your street today."

"Oh," said Mary Jane. "I'd better put Mother's perfume away." She put the stopper in the bottle and put the bottle in its place. She was none too soon.

Mary Jane heard the sound of a key in the front door. She picked up the cat and ran downstairs. Her mother came puffing into the house with two large bags of groceries.

When Mrs. Brooks saw the cat, she put the bags on the floor. "Mary Jane, I've told you not to bring cats into the house. Take it back where it belongs."

Mary Jane watched her mother put away the groceries. She was glad to see three new cans of tuna fish.

Mary Jane's mother was folding the empty grocery bags. "Oh, dear, I'll never get the house tidy before your father comes home. Here, put the bags away."

"I can't take the cat back, Mother." Mary Jane took the bags. "It's a witch's cat. She flew away on a vacuum cleaner, and left the cat here."

"Vacuum cleaner!" said Mary Jane's mother. "Mary Jane, could you vacuum the rug?"

While Mary Jane went to get the vacuum cleaner, Mrs. Brooks went into the living room with a dustcloth, and the cat followed her. Mrs. Brooks was about to dust a vase when she saw the cat jump to the mantelpiece and walk softly to the tall silver candlestick beside the clock. The cat dusted it carefully with her tail and swished away the dust around it.

Moving to the clock she dusted that too. She gave a few expert flicks of her tail to the candlestick on the other side of the clock and leaped to the bookcase to dust a little china lady and a glass bowl. Mrs. Brooks put down the vase. The cat walked over to it, swished her tail up and around the vase, and jumped to the floor. Then she looked at Mary Jane's mother with big sad eyes. Dusting was not something Mrs. Brooks enjoyed. This cat seemed to love it. For a long time Mary Jane's mother just stood there. At last she said, "Are you *sure* that cat doesn't belong to anyone?"

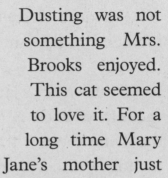

By this time Mary Jane was running the vacuum cleaner. She had to shout to make herself heard over the sound of the motor. "Oh, she belongs to the witch."

Mrs. Brooks turned off the vacuum cleaner. "Mary Jane, I've told you so many times not to make up stories. Does the cat have a name?"

"The witch calls her 'Hey, you!' "

After a moment's thought Mary Jane's mother announced, "I'm going to call her 'Cinders' because she does the work like Cinderella. Poor thing, she is much too thin."

MAGIC SCISSORS

While Mary Jane and her mother were making friends with the cat, Witch Hilda was flying home as fast as she could. The jug of the vacuum cleaner was not a comfortable seat, but Hilda was used to it. She pointed the metal wand in front of her and steered.

This had not been a good Wednesday. The witch was angry at the little girl for not opening the door. She did not know why she had wanted so much to get into that house, except that it smelled so strongly of mischief. Now Hilda was eager to be home. She wanted to begin work on a new kind of spell.

She was flying above a bank of pink sunset clouds. Night would soon fall.

Hilda gave a cry of wild witch joy. Then she began to sing in her harsh voice:

Oh, give me the life of a bat
When the shades of night come down.
I fly with my little black cat
To the dear old witches' town.

Cat? Hilda looked down at her lap. No cat. She looked at the metal wand. No cat. She even closed one eye and squinted up the thick hose. Still no cat. "Drat!" said the witch.

As she neared Witch Town, Hilda licked her lips at the thought of the pot of brew bubbling in her cave. "I'll look for the cat after supper," she said.

Hilda lived in a large cave in the side of a mountain. Nearby were many other caves and shacks where witches lived. The smoke from their bonfires rose out of the dark woods, and sounds of chanting came from groups of witches sitting around huge black pots.

The weary witch flew straight to her own cave with only a nod to some friends. She left the vacuum cleaner in the middle of the floor. It was too much bother to put it away.

She grabbed a spoon and went to the black iron pot in the corner. What a shame! The fire was out, and the brew was cold. Hilda felt like crying.

There was no little cat to send for firewood, so Hilda had to go herself. She found only a few twigs. The other witches had taken most of the wood. "Drat," said Hilda, "why must they all build fires tonight?" In the end Witch Hilda had a cold snack of grasshopper legs. She went to bed hungry and in no mood to look for the cat.

Next morning it rained. The witch climbed up on a high stool and took down

an old black book. The pages were yellow, dog-eared, and spotted. Hilda liked to study the book while having her cup of witch's brew.

She licked her finger and turned the pages. "Salts, sandwiches, scissors!" The witch read the recipe for scissors twice and went to work. The recipe called for octopus eyelashes, among other things.

The vacuum cleaner did a lot of flying that week while the witch collected what she needed. By Sunday night Hilda had everything the recipe called for. All Monday and Tuesday she dropped things into the big black pot and sang strange and terrible songs. At noon on Wednesday she dipped her big spoon into the hissing brew. Down at the bottom she found what she wanted. She fished out a little pair of pointed scissors.

Hilda smiled. She looked at the sun.

"Late. It's Wednesday, and it's late. I must hurry."

She jumped on the vacuum cleaner and ordered, "Mischief, James."

The vacuum cleaner whirred and wobbled. With a bounce it jumped into the air and sailed out of the cave into the sunshine. Hilda held tight to the sides of the jug. Her round body bobbed up and down with the motion of the vacuum cleaner. In her hurry she had forgotten to take off her apron. She dropped the scissors into the apron pocket.

Hilda pointed the rod straight ahead

and gave the jug a kick to make it go faster. Wednesday was more than half over. If she wanted any fun she would have to be quick.

"I wonder where James is taking me," thought the witch. She had been traveling for some time. The ground below looked familiar. The vacuum cleaner glided down and landed on a walk leading to a white house. "This must be where I lost the cat." Hilda climbed off the jug, shook out her black skirt, gathered up the vacuum cleaner, and clumped up the steps of the house.

She rang the bell and waited. The cover to the peep hole moved, and someone looked out. "I'm looking for a cat," said Hilda. "Have you seen one?"

"What sort of cat?" growled a deep voice.

"Black," replied the witch.

"Oh, you could hardly call our cat black."

This was true. Mary Jane and Cinders had been going through Mrs. Brooks's dressing table while Mary Jane's mother was at the post office. Cinders had knocked over a box of bath powder and was now a strange shade of gray. Mary Jane could hear her sneezing.

The witch also heard her. "That sounds like my cat," she said. "Let me see it."

"I can't let anyone in," said Mary Jane.

Just then Mrs. Brooks came up the walk carrying a large package. She laid it down when she saw the witch on her doorstep. "I'm glad you came so quickly. I see you've brought a new one. It's a bit different from mine, but anything would be better. Come in." She picked up James and rang the doorbell. "Open up, Mary

Jane. This lady brought us a new vacuum cleaner. That's fast service. I telephoned only this morning to tell them ours isn't working very well."

Mary Jane opened the door and was face to face with the witch. Hilda's green eyes looked into Mary Jane's brown ones. "She's not very big," thought Hilda, "but she certainly smells of mischief."

Mary Jane's mother could also smell something. She ran upstairs so fast that she forgot to put  down the vacuum cleaner. She found Cinders in a pile of white powder, coughing and sneezing. Cinders looked so funny Mrs. Brooks had to laugh even though she was angry with Mary Jane. Then she plugged in the vacuum cleaner and cleaned up the mess.

Poor James was not used to being used as a vacuum cleaner. The bath powder was choking him.

Downstairs Hilda was upset. Time was wasting. "You know it's my cat." Hilda glared at Mary Jane, who glared back at her.

"She wants to live with me. Can't you get another cat?"

"This one suits me," said the witch. "I'm going to take her home with me."

Mrs. Brooks came downstairs, carrying the dusty little cat. When Cinders saw the witch she drew back against Mary Jane's mother and tried to hide in her clothes.

"That's my cat," said Hilda sharply. "I lost her a week ago."

"We have become very fond of Cinders," Mrs. Brooks said gently. "Won't you let us buy her from you?"

"No," said Hilda. "I need her."

Mary Jane's mother sadly handed the trembling little cat to the witch. "Just a minute," she said, "I'll give you the old vacuum cleaner. You can send me a bill for the new one."

Hilda was handed the Brookses' worn-out vacuum cleaner and gently but firmly pushed out the door.

"Drat!" said the witch. "Now I'll have to walk home." She looked angrily at the cat. "It's all your fault. Well, I won't have you getting lost again." She pulled the scissors from her pocket.

Holding the cat by the scruff of the neck, the witch snipped her with the magic scissors. Cinders grew smaller and smaller and smaller. The scissors did not hurt. What they snipped did not fall to the ground or blow away in the wind. The magic scissors made things smaller but did not change their shape in any way.

When Hilda stopped cutting, the cat

was only one inch high. She could fit nicely in a walnut shell. And yet she was exactly like the big Cinders. Each tiny whisker was perfect. Her yellow eyes gleamed just as they always had, but now they were the size of the beads on Mrs. Brooks's evening bag, the one Mary Jane was going through when the bath powder had spilled on Cinders.

Hilda held the cat on the palm of her hand. "Beautiful! If I say it myself," she cackled.

The witch snipped the old vacuum cleaner until it was only big enough for a dollhouse. She caught sight of the package Mrs. Brooks left on the steps. She thought of snipping it small too, but she decided to unwrap it instead. The package was packed in cardboard and straw and tied with strong cord. When Hilda tried to cut the cord with her scissors it got smaller and tighter without being cut in two. The witch chewed through the cord. Cinders was now too small to help.

When the string was off, Hilda tore open the box. She found a dollhouse, quite a nice one but not what she was looking for. She was going to kick it when she saw something in the corner of the bottom step, something that shone in the fading light.

It was a pair of roller skates. Mary Jane had left them on the step. Now *these* would be more useful. The witch sat down and strapped on the skates. "I'll improve them when I get home, but for now they're better than nothing."

She dropped the tiny cat into her apron pocket. "There you are. Now, hold tight, and we'll soon be home where you can have some nice witch's brew."

Cinders thought about the witch's brew and then about the tuna fish and chicken and leftover gravy in Mary Jane's house. She dug her claws into the apron and climbed to the top of the pocket. There she clung for a moment. When Hilda bent over to tighten a skate strap, Cinders leaped quietly to the grass near the front walk.

It was dark now. The witch did not see the tiny cat slip into the shadows.

Hilda had not skated for years, and she wondered if she still could. She tried—first one foot, then the other. It was just as thrilling as she remembered. Hilda glided down the walk to the street, and then faster and faster she skated, guided by her sharp nose. Far off she could smell the pots of Witch Town.

When she had gone, Cinders ran into the dollhouse. Everything in it was just the right size for her. She curled up in the corner of the tiny living room sofa and went to sleep.

THE DOLLHOUSE

Mary Jane followed her mother upstairs to get the vacuum cleaner. They were both sad because the witch had taken Cinders, but Mary Jane still had hope. After all they did have James, the magic vacuum cleaner.

The vacuum cleaner was in Mrs. Brooks's bedroom, feeling sick with all the bath powder in it. "Mother," said Mary Jane, "let me clean the jug."

"It doesn't need cleaning. It's brand new."

"No, it isn't. The witch has been using it."

"The witch? Oh, you mean that funny little woman who took Cinders away. Hmmm. Let me see that vacuum cleaner.

Mary Jane, you're right! It isn't new at all. Look at all those dents and scratches! I'll have to telephone the company and complain."

Mary Jane didn't think that would be the right thing to do. "Mother," she said, "maybe this is a trade for our old one. Why don't we see how well it works, and do let me clean it out."

"Oh, all right," said Mrs. Brooks. "But be careful carrying it downstairs."

Mary Jane took James downstairs and out the front door to the garbage can under the steps.

Her mother came after her. "Mary Jane, is that package still there? Aunt Harriet sent it to you from England. It's a late birthday present."

Mrs. Brooks stared at the litter of torn paper and cardboard around the dollhouse. "Oh, you've opened it. You should have waited until we had it in the house."

Mary Jane was sure it was the witch who had opened the package, but she said nothing.

James felt much better. He wiggled in Mary Jane's kind arms, and she patted him to make him stay still. Her mother would have to take an aspirin and lie down if she saw James do anything peculiar. Mary Jane hurried upstairs with James and hid him in her closet.

"Hurry, Mary Jane," called Mrs. Brooks. "Help me bring in the dollhouse."

Mary Jane grabbed one end of the dollhouse. Her mother took the other. Together they carried it into the house.

It was a slow hard trip upstairs with the dollhouse. They had trouble getting it around the corner at the landing. When they reached the top of the stairs, they carried it down the hall to Mary Jane's room.

"We can put it on top of your dresser,"

Mrs. Brooks said. "Run and get a dust-cloth. I do wish Cinders were here!"

Any other time Mary Jane would have been wild with joy over a dollhouse like this with a stairway and a complete set of furniture. Now she hardly looked at it. Cinders was gone. Mary Jane wanted to cry.

Mary Jane dusted the dresser, and they lifted the dollhouse onto it.

Mrs. Brooks looked at her watch. "Goodness, it's late. I'd like to help you arrange the furniture, but I don't have time. I must get supper before Daddy comes home. Now, remember to write a thank-you letter to Aunt Harriet."

She hurried downstairs. Mary Jane sat on a chair in front of the dollhouse and looked in. She had never seen one like it. There were little electric lights that worked—only now they needed a battery. The furniture was packed carefully in newspaper and wedged into the rooms. Some of the furniture was not completely wrapped. Mary Jane could see the seat cushions of the chairs and the sheets and blankets on the beds. One little sofa was hardly wrapped at all. Curled up in the corner was a tiny black cat.

Mary Jane lifted the sofa out of the dollhouse and looked at the cat. "English toys seem so real," she thought. "This looks exactly like Cinders." A tear rolled down Mary Jane's nose and fell with a splash on the little cat. The cat jumped to its feet and opened its eyes wide.

"It's raining!" said Cinders. "Where am I?"

Her voice was so small that Mary Jane had to strain her ears to hear. She lifted the cat to her face and examined her. "You look just like Cinders—only smaller."

"And you look like Mary Jane—only bigger."

"Oh, Cinders, it is you!" Mary Jane jumped with excitement.

"Don't drop me!" cried the cat. "It's a long way down."

"What happened to you?"

"The witch thought I'd be easier to carry if I were small. Her scissors make things small without hurting them."

Mary Jane heard her father's voice. "Mary Jane, don't leave your toys in the front yard. Come and get this."

Mary Jane put Cinders back in the dollhouse and ran to greet her father. He hugged her and then handed her a little vacuum cleaner. "Don't be so careless, Mary Jane. I found this on the front walk. That's a good way to lose your things."

Mary Jane remembered the skates. She went outside to look for them. She looked in the bushes and all around the walk. "Maybe I'll find them tomorrow morning," she told herself. "It's too dark now."

During supper Mary Jane slipped a bit of lamb chop into her pocket. Luckily neither her mother nor her father saw her do it.

After Mary Jane and her mother had washed the dishes and put them away, Mrs. Brooks said, "Let's show Daddy the dollhouse Aunt Harriet sent you from England."

"I don't have the furniture set up yet."

"Never mind." Her mother took off her apron. "We'll help you."

Mary Jane's mother and father crowded into her room and stood in front of the dresser to look at the dollhouse. Mary Jane saw Cinders curled up on the rug in front of the little fireplace. She quickly cupped her hand over the cat, scooped her up, and dropped her into her pocket—the one with the piece of lamb chop.

Cinders was hungry. It was hard to eat such a big piece of meat. She pulled and tore at it with her sharp teeth. It was like eating in a hammock. Cinder kept rolling over. In her efforts to right herself, she dug her claws right through the dress into Mary Jane.

"Ouch!" said Mary Jane.

Mr. Brooks was setting up the bathroom while Mrs. Brooks fussed with the ruffles of the tiny four-poster bed. "What's the matter, Mary Jane?" he asked. "You're jumping about as if you had fleas."

Mary Jane went to her desk and put Cinders and the meat in the top drawer. She left it open a crack for air.

Her mother and father were admiring the tiny set of dishes and the pots and pans. "I hope you'll take good care of this, Mary Jane," said her father. "Aunt Harriet must have paid a lot of money for it."

Mary Jane's parents seemed to like the dollhouse just as much as she did. They did not go downstairs until they had unpacked everything and arranged the furniture. The only thing missing was a doll. Mary Jane had none the right size.

"Where's that little vacuum cleaner?" asked Mr. Brooks.

"I left it downstairs." Mary Jane brought it up and gave it to her father.

"This is the nicest piece of all," he said.

Mrs. Brooks looked at it and turned pale. "I think I'll take an aspirin and lie down."

HOMEWORK

When her parents had gone, Mary Jane took Cinders out of the drawer. The drawer was a bit greasy from Cinders' tussle with the piece of lamb chop. Mary Jane gave the cat a drink of water in a soda-bottle cap, and Cinders smoothed her whiskers and sighed contentedly. "I'm glad the witch didn't take me home with her. I would have had witch's brew for supper. Do you know what's in that brew, Mary Jane?"

Mary Jane shook her head. She sat on her bed and put Cinders on her shoulder, close to her ear. Mary Jane loved to hear about the witch and her doings.

"Well," said Cinders, settling herself

against Mary Jane's collar, "the witch does all her magic with that brew. When she wants to put something under a spell she finds a recipe in an old book of hers. She adds the things in the recipe to whatever is in the pot. There's everything from old suspenders to poison ivy in there. And she expects me to drink it!"

"Poor Cinders! Was that how she made the magic scissors?"

"Of course," replied the cat. "Did you know she cut down your old vacuum cleaner?"

"Yes, my mother was upset when she saw it. Magic makes her ill."

Mary Jane was reminded of James. She went to the closet and pulled him out. "Does James miss the witch?"

"Oh, no, she used to kick him. You can see the marks."

"Does he need anything?"

"He likes to travel. Don't keep him cooped up. Do you have time for a trip this evening?"

Mary Jane caught her breath with excitement. She tried to sound calm. "Just a short one. My mother might miss me."

Cinders loved to ride the vacuum cleaner. "Open the window," she ordered, "and get the hose and wand."

"The wand? Oh, you mean that stick thing."

The hose and wand were still in her mother's room. Mary Jane tip-toed down the hall and got them.

"Put me on top of your head," said Cinders. Mary Jane put the little cat on her head. "Now wind the hose around your neck. Did you notice how Witch Hilda did it?"

The vacuum-cleaner hose was hard to keep in place. Mary Jane grabbed it with one hand and held the wand in the other. She opened the window and sat down on James.

"Point the wand where you want to go and steer with it."

"Fly, James." Mary Jane pointed the wand at the open window.

The vacuum cleaner rose with a wobble, then became more steady and glided out the window. Mary Jane held the wand straight in front of her. Wherever she pointed it the vacuum cleaner flew—up, down, around a corner. As she passed the window of her friend Marian's house she saw Marian doing her homework.

"Oops!" said Mary Jane. "Home, James."

She flew in her own window just in time. Her mother was coming upstairs. Mary Jane pushed the vacuum cleaner into her closet and sat down at her desk. She took Cinders out of her hair, put her gently in the desk drawer, and dropped a piece of Kleenex in with her. "Try to clean up the mess in there," she whispered. "My pencils will smell of lamb chop."

"Mary Jane, have you started your homework?" called her mother.

"Almost." Mary Jane shut the desk drawer to a crack and opened a book.

Mrs. Brooks came in. "I've brought you a glass of milk and some crackers."

"Great!" said Mary Jane.

Her mother looked at her. "Well?"

"Thank you," Mary Jane said.

"Now, get busy." Mrs. Brooks went out and quietly shut the door.

Mary Jane was studying her spelling. Cinders was a great help with spelling. She read the words aloud, and Mary Jane wrote them down. Mary Jane poured some milk into the soda-bottle cap and set it in the drawer. "Will you help me with my homework when you've finished, Cinders?"

The cat lifted a black face with milky

whiskers. "I'll try sitting on your shoulder to read. The letters are very big for me now."

Cinders helped Mary Jane with the spelling, showed her some quick tricks with arithmetic, and listened to her read. Soon the homework was done. Mary Jane noticed that the little cat was yawning. "Would you like to go to bed, Cinders? The basket you slept in yesterday is too big now."

"If you don't mind, I'd like to look around the dollhouse."

Mary Jane put the cat in the dollhouse. It was now neat and perfectly furnished. Cinders walked from room to room. She jumped on the red velvet chair to test how soft it was. She nodded to herself in the long mirror. She looked with disgust at the toy food. A little set of dishes charmed her. Mary Jane went to get some butter to put on a doll's plate. She filled a tiny bowl with cream—it didn't take much.

Cinders ran her pink tongue round and round the bowl. "In some ways I rather like being this size." When she finished her snack she ran through the house, scampered up the little stairway, and jumped into the four-poster bed. She wiggled under the covers and peeked out from between the curtains. "Good night, Mary Jane. See you in the morning."

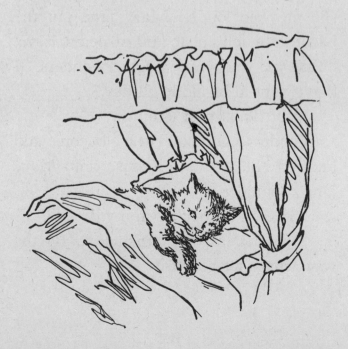

Cinders in School

In the morning rush to get ready for school, Mary Jane hardly had time to give Cinders breakfast. She ran upstairs with a scrap of bacon in her napkin. Cinders was prowling hungrily around the dollhouse kitchen. When she saw Mary Jane she meowed loudly. Mary Jane put the bacon on a doll's plate and turned to leave. "Take me with you," begged Cinders. "I don't want to be alone all day."

"But I'm almost late now."

Cinders gobbled the bacon and jumped out of the dollhouse onto Mary Jane's shoulder.

"There's no pocket in my dress."

"I'll ride in your lunch box. By the way, what's for lunch?"

"A roast-beef sandwich, and you'd better go in the pencil case."

"I don't like pencils, and I'd be crowded."

Mary Jane was firm. "I'll put the pencils in the lunch box and you in the pencil case."

Cinders sighed. Mary Jane didn't seem to trust her. Still, she would probably give her a little of the roast beef at lunch time.

"Hurry, Mary Jane," called Mrs. Brooks. Mary Jane put her pencils into her lunch box and pushed Cinders into the pencil case. She picked up her books and ran down the stairs and out the front door.

As she clattered down the front steps she called back over her shoulder, "Mother, look for my roller skates, will you?"

Hearing a thumping in the pencil case, Mary Jane opened it a crack. "What's the matter?"

Cinders put her mouth to the crack and yelled, "I forgot to tell you. The witch took your skates."

"Well, *I* have the magic vacuum cleaner. It's a good trade." Mary Jane stopped talking and began to run. Hot and panting for breath, she reached the school yard and got in line just as the children were going into the school.

She put the pencil case into her desk, but Cinders started thumping again. Mary Jane bent over and whispered, "What is it?"

"Let me out. I'll just stay in the desk."

Mary Jane saw the teacher, Mrs. Carson, looking at her. She didn't dare argue with Cinders. Reaching into her desk she opened the pencil case.

"Mary Jane," said Mrs. Carson, "what is in your desk?"

"My pencil case, Mrs. Carson."

Mrs. Carson smiled the cold smile of a teacher who has caught a pupil in a crime. She walked over to Mary Jane's desk and held out her hand. "Let me see the pencil case."

Mary Jane reached into the desk. Something small and furry ran up her arm onto her shoulder and hid under her hair. It tickled. Mary Jane didn't dare to giggle. She handed Mrs. Carson the pencil case.

The teacher opened the case. "What else is in your desk?"

"Nothing, Mrs. Carson."

Mrs. Carson was a short, heavy woman. She always had the children pick up the chalk if she dropped it. No one had ever seen her bend over to look into a desk. The whole class watched. Mrs. Carson fooled them. "Give me your seat, Mary Jane." Mary Jane moved into the aisle and let Mrs. Carson take her place. She stuck her hand in the desk but found nothing.

"When she goes back to the front of the room," whispered a small voice, "lean over your book."

The teacher stood up. She was still sure Mary Jane was up to something. "Very well, leave the pencil case alone and get to work."

"Yes, Mrs. Carson."

When the teacher returned to her own desk, she was pleased to see Mary Jane leaning over a book. Cinders jumped through the hole in the desk top. The hole had been made for an inkwell, but there was no ink in it. The children used ball-point pens.

The cat was hidden. Mary Jane hoped she would stay quiet.

Mrs. Carson was giving a lesson in arithmetic. "Now, children, if John had eleven apples and Sue had six, how many did they have together?" Mary Jane did not raise her hand, so the teacher called on her. "How many, Mary Jane?"

"Eighteen," said Mary Jane.

"Seventeen, silly!" said Cinders.

"I mean seventeen," Mary Jane said.

Mrs. Carson looked around the room. "Did I hear someone helping Mary Jane?"

All the children were quiet. Mrs. Carson glared at each face in turn. "Don't do it again," she said to the class. "Sit down, Mary Jane."

"She's meaner than the witch," said Cinders.

At twelve o'clock the children went to the basement lunch room. Mary Jane carried Cinders in her lunch box. The sandwich was in a plastic bag. Marian came to sit with her.

"Hi, Marian," said Mary Jane, opening her lunch box and pulling Cinders out of her sandwich. Cinders had bitten through the plastic bag and was pulling the meat out of the bread. Mary Jane put a bit of meat and the cat back in the lunch box and closed the lid.

Marian had opened her mouth to take a bite of her own sandwich and left it open when she saw the tiny cat.

"What's the matter, Marian?" Mary Jane took a big bite of roast beef and bread.

"I thought I saw a cat."

"Oh, that's Cinders. She didn't want

to stay home alone so I brought her in my pencil case. I wish I hadn't."

"I thought there was something funny going on. Carsey nearly caught you."

The lunch box rattled. Mary Jane opened it. Cinders jumped up on the thermos bottle. "That teacher is worse than the witch."

Marian stared. Before she had not been able to believe her eyes. Now her ears were playing tricks. "The witch?" she asked.

"Remember?" said Mary Jane. "I told you about it."

"I thought it was just one of your stories."

Mary Jane glared. "You didn't believe me. You're just like my mother."

Marian was over her surprise. "I thought she was a regular-sized cat."

"The witch snipped her small with a pair of magic scissors."

"And I'm getting mighty tired of it," said Cinders, arching her back. "I can't stay home alone all day. Your mother might step on me. She's nearsighted. She'd think I was a water bug."

"But, Cinders, you make such a lot of trouble in school. Couldn't you go to sleep?"

"Maybe if I had a nice drink of milk. Open your thermos."

"What will you drink out of?"

"Pour some milk in your hand for me."

This was sloppy, and when Cinders had drunk her fill Mary Jane dried her hand on the paper napkin her mother had packed. Then she made a nest of Kleenex in the lunch box for the cat.

Mary Jane drank the rest of her milk and crunched her way through an apple. She traded two sugar cookies for a big, puffy, chocolate-coated marshmallow one of Marian's. As she nibbled the cookie, Mary Jane told about yesterday's adventures. "I'm trying to figure a way both you and I can ride the vacuum cleaner," she finished.

The lunch box rattled. Mary Jane opened it. "Mary Jane," said Cinders snappishly, "if you'd ask me I'd tell you."

"How?" Mary Jane leaned over until her nose nearly touched the tiny furry animal.

"Don't do that, Mary Jane! You're so big that it scares me."

Mary Jane moved back. "Well, how, Cinders, how?"

The cat curled into a sleepy ball on her nest of Kleenex. "I'll tell you tomorrow." She closed her yellow eyes.

Mary Jane shut the box. "I hope she sleeps all afternoon."

The girls sat close together on the

bench. "You really flew past my window last night?" asked Marian.

"You were doing your homework. It reminded me I hadn't done mine."

A stout woman in a white apron moved about, cleaning the tables. Mary Jane set her lunch box on her lap. Children's voices echoed off the walls. She wondered how Cinders could sleep with all the din.

In the afternoon they had reading and spelling. Mary Jane was glad Cinders was asleep. The cat could read and spell better than anyone in the class. And she was such a show-off.

It was a long hot afternoon. Outside the window the sky was very blue. There was the sound of men working in the street. Mary Jane hated the terrible rattle of the air hammers. There were two more weeks of school before the summer vacation. She could hardly wait.

After school she walked home with

Marian. "It's so hot," said Marian. "Don't you wish we could go to the beach?"

Mary Jane picked a dandelion that had gone to seed. "The beach. I wonder if we could." She blew the seeds away and watched them fly on their feathery down. "I'll ask Cinders tomorrow."

"Why tomorrow?"

"Cinders said she'd tell me tomorrow how to ride two on the magic vacuum cleaner. Tomorrow is Friday, and the day after is Saturday and—"

Marian understood. "Saturday," she said, "we could go for a picnic."

THE PLAN

On Friday Cinders slept late. Mary Jane left the cat's breakfast in the dollhouse and went off without her. After school she spent a moment in the kitchen before going upstairs. When Cinders saw Mary Jane she jumped off the little sofa and began meowing loudly. "It was so lonely without you, and I'm hungry."

Mary Jane pulled a sardine tail from her pocket. "I thought you might be. I stopped in the kitchen to get this."

When she had finished eating, Cinders washed her face. "If you plan to ride the vacuum cleaner to the beach," she said, "you'd better get a map. James goes only where you steer him."

"Can he carry two?" asked Mary Jane.

"Yes, if one of you rides the hose."

This seemed simple. Mary Jane put Cinders on her shoulder and went downstairs. Cinders hid under Mary Jane's collar. "Mother, I need a road map that shows the way to the beach."

"Homework, I suppose," said Mrs. Brooks. "Look in the kitchen drawer."

Mary Jane began to explore the drawer. Under the gardening book with beautiful flowers on the cover were books of saving stamps. The stamp books were so interesting that Mary Jane almost forgot what she was looking for. She dug down through bits of string, a Christmas-tree ornament, a wooden spoon. Finally, at the bottom, Mary Jane found several road maps. She unfolded one and tried to read it, but she couldn't tell the way to the beach.

"Ask your mother," whispered Cinders.

Mrs. Brooks was making a meat loaf.

When she turned away from it to help Mary Jane, Cinders ran down Mary Jane's arm and jumped onto the table. She grabbed a mouthful of meat and sprang into Mary Jane's pocket. This was done so quickly that Mary Jane hardly believed it happened. Her mother didn't see it at all.

Mary Jane's mother marked a path on the map with a red crayon. "This map only shows the main streets. Our street would be about here." She made an X on the map.

"Suppose you were flying, Mother, starting from my window, which way would you go?"

"From your window I'd take a short cut over the apartment building, past your school, and down to the park. Then I'd follow Ocean Parkway—that's the street with the double rows of trees. When you reach the Belt Parkway, swing to the left and follow the shore. There are lots of beaches on Long Island. You might even fly as far as Montauk. It's lovely there. If you were in a hurry you could just go down Ocean Parkway to Brighton Beach or Coney Island."

Mary Jane wished magic didn't make her mother sick. It would be fun to tell her everything.

"Talking of the beach, Mary Jane," said Mrs. Brooks, "see if you can find the swimming mask. I have to chop onions."

Mrs. Brooks wore the swimming mask to keep from crying when she chopped onions. It made her look very strange.

Mary Jane had seen the mask in the kitchen drawer. She pulled it out from under two aprons and an electric cord.

"With the right recipe," said Cinders, from Mary Jane's pocket, "you could do magic with that drawer."

"Shh!" said Mary Jane, and left the kitchen.

The doorbell rang. Mary Jane climbed on a chair to look through the peep hole. Marian was standing on the doorstep.

Marian saw the bright brown eye through the peep hole. "Let me in," she said in a raspy voice. "I am a wicked witch."

Mary Jane opened the door. "Come upstairs. I'll show you the dollhouse."

When Marian saw the dollhouse she began to move the furniture around. Mary Jane put Cinders in the living room. The cat was about to jump into the red chair by the fireplace when Marian moved it. Cinders let out a yowl—as loud as she could with her tiny lungs.

"Mary Jane," howled the cat, "make her stop messing up my house!"

"Dollhouses are meant to be played with," said Marian.

"Not *my* house!" Cinders stretched out on the sofa.

Mary Jane was dragging James out of the closet. "Look, Marian!"

"It looks like an ordinary old vacuum cleaner." Marian sniffed.

Mary Jane sat on the vacuum cleaner. She wrapped the hose around her neck and picked up the wand. "Once around the room, James."

James was not used to such cramped space. He got off to a wobbly start and then curved sharply to turn the corner of the room. Mary Jane's legs caught in a chair and overturned it with a crash. This startled James. He rose sharply. Mary Jane's head hit the ceiling with a bang. For a moment she was stunned and let the wand point downward. Down zoomed James like a dive bomber. By this time Marian was crawling under the bed.

"What's going on up there?" called Mrs. Brooks.

"I knocked over a chair!" yelled Mary

Jane. "Down, James!" she said hoarsely, pointing the wand at the floor. James came to a quivering stop.

"Have you finished flying?" asked Marian from under the bed.

"For now," said Mary Jane, "but I'm taking you to the beach tomorrow. Remember?"

"I'm trying to forget," said her friend in a weak voice.

"It's very simple," said Mary Jane, "you just have to straddle the hose and hang on to it— like riding a snake."

Marian looked doubtful. "I never rode a snake."

"Practice makes perfect," said a voice from the dollhouse.

"Cinders," asked Mary Jane, "will you come on the trip?"

"I don't care for swimming," said the cat, "but I'll go for the ride, and don't forget to pack lunch."

THE PICNIC

Saturday was sunny. The girls asked their mothers if they could have a picnic. Mary Jane's mother was happy to find a use for yesterday's leftovers. She made meat-loaf sandwiches and filled a thermos bottle with lemonade. Marian's mother gave her a box of cookies and two big yellow apples. By half past nine everything was ready.

Carrying a shopping bag, Mary Jane and Marian went to get the vacuum cleaner. Marian had her bathing suit, and Mary Jane found hers in her bottom drawer. She crammed both suits into the shopping bag with the food.

Cinders was asleep in the doll's four-poster bed. Mary Jane gently pulled back the covers and lifted the tiny black ball of fur to her face. The cat opened a yellow eye and asked, "Is it time for breakfast?"

"We've had ours. I'd better give you some meat loaf." Mary Jane unpacked a sandwich. She had to unpack the bathing suits first. She served Cinders a bit of meat loaf on a doll's plate. Cinders asked for a second helping. Mary Jane had to unpack the sandwich again.

"Are you sure you've had enough?"

"I think I'd like a little milk, if it's not too much trouble."

Mary Jane took a thimble down to the kitchen and filled it with milk. She spilled some. It is hard to pour milk into a thimble.

"Have you seen the vacuum cleaner anywhere, Mary Jane?" asked Mrs. Brooks. "I want to vacuum the living room."

"I'm going to be using it. I'll give it to you when I've finished."

"Your room really is a mess. I'm glad you're going to clean it up. Aren't you going for a picnic?"

"Yes," said Mary Jane. She carried the thimbleful of milk upstairs and poured it in a doll's bowl. "Hurry, Cinders. My mother wants to use the vacuum cleaner."

"That's bad. James hates dust." The cat began to lap the milk.

Mary Jane connected the hose to the vacuum cleaner and unfolded the map. "You'd better hang on to the shopping bag, Marian. I have to steer."

Cinders had finished her milk. "I'll ride on your shoulder, near your ear."

Mary Jane opened the window and picked up the metal wand. With the shopping bag handles looped over her arm, Marian straddled the hose and held on with both hands.

"Ready?" asked Cinders.

"As ready as I'll ever be," said Marian.

"To the beach, James," said Mary Jane. She pointed the wand at the open window.

James liked Mary Jane because she never kicked him. Yesterday he had been out of practice. Today he meant to give her a smooth ride. Carefully he rose into the air. The hose stretched out behind like a tail. Marian hung on, and the whole picnic party sailed out the window into the June sunshine.

Mary Jane held the map open. It flapped in the breeze and made it hard to steer. As James zoomed over the apartment building, a small boy was looking out the window. He told his mother what he saw, but she didn't believe him. Soon the vacuum cleaner was high in the air. From the ground it looked like a strange kite.

They sailed past the school and over the park. Soon they flew over the wide street with the double rows of trees.

Marian was having trouble. Her feet kept flipping out behind her. The string handles of the heavy shopping bag cut into her arm. When she looked down she grew dizzy. "Mary Jane, aren't we almost there?"

"Almost. We should be coming to the highway soon."

Cinders had forgotten how much fun it was to fly. The wind blew through her ears and tail. She clung with sharp little claws to Mary Jane's polo shirt. Both girls were wearing jeans. Mary Jane thought they were better for flying than skirts, although, as Cinders pointed out, the witch never wore jeans.

They reached the Belt Parkway. In front of them the sea sparkled. Mary Jane steered toward it. She flew along the coast until Brighton Beach and Coney Island were far behind. Now there were fewer houses. They flew over a wild area with no roads leading to the shore. The narrow beach was deserted.

A sea gull swooped and screamed. James flew right over the water. Far below was the white sail of a boat. Marian was so frightened at the sight of the ocean below her that she nearly lost her grip. "Turn back, Mary Jane!" she cried.

Mary Jane swung the vacuum cleaner around and pointed down to the beach. They landed in a cloud of flying sand. Marian rolled over and over.

Mary Jane gave James a pat. "Isn't this great?"

Marian grunted and blew the sand off her mouth.

The sun and sand were warm. In the shelter of a clump of scrubby bushes poking up from the sand dunes, the girls changed into their bathing suits. They left their clothes near the vacuum cleaner and the shopping bag. Cinders asked to be put

into the shopping bag. "The sun hurts my eyes," she explained.

The girls raced across the shining sand and splashed up to their ankles in the cold sea. Their toes sank in the wet sand as a wave drew back. Another wave rolled in and wet them to their knees. Leaning over they dipped their arms in the water. Pebbles and shells of many colors were at the bottom. Marian fished up a piece of dark seaweed, which was covered with strange pods like little green bubbles.

After a while they sat at the water's edge and let the waves splash over them. The sea no longer seemed cold. Marian built a castle in the wet sand. Mary Jane helped by cleaning the sand out of the moat as it fell in.

Their stomachs told them when it was time for lunch. When they unpacked the shopping bag in the shade of a bush, Cinders was found in a plastic sandwich bag. She had eaten a surprising amount of the sandwich filling. Marian looked at the sandwich and made a face. "You can have this one, Mary Jane."

Mary Jane uncorked the thermos. Little pieces of ice tinkled in the lemonade. The paper cups were mashed but still usable. It was a delightful picnic. Only Cinders complained. She didn't like lemonade. "It's not as bad as witch's brew," she said politely, "but I'd rather have cream, or even milk, if you're out of cream."

After lunch Cinders went to sleep in the shopping bag. Mary Jane and Marian took turns burying each other in the sand. The afternoon sun made them drowsy, and soon they too curled up on the beach and fell asleep.

Marian woke when a wave crept to her feet. The tide was coming in. She was stiff from sleeping on the ground, and her mouth was dry and salty. The vacuum cleaner was already deep in the water. At any minute it might be washed away. Marian got to her feet and shook Mary Jane.

For a moment Mary Jane did not know where she was. Remembering, she jumped up and dragged the vacuum cleaner to a place the tide had not yet reached. Their clothes and the shopping bag were wet through. Mary Jane looked frantically for Cinders. At last she saw her, crawling through the sand. The tiny cat had left the shopping bag when the water had begun to seep in.

The shopping bag was a wreck. They put their clothes on over their bathing suits. Wet socks and shoes were nasty to put on, and it took a while to get dressed. The wet clothes felt good on their sunburned shoulders.

When they were ready, Cinders clung to Mary Jane's soggy shoulder. "I almost miss the witch. *She* never did things like this."

Seated on the vacuum cleaner, Mary Jane waited until Marian had a firm grip on the hose and then pointed the wand skyward. "Home, James!"

The map had fallen apart in the sea water, but Mary Jane was sure she remembered the way home. They flew inland until they saw the highway, but where was the street with the double rows of trees?

"What's the matter?" asked Cinders. Mary Jane had steered the vacuum cleaner in a circle for the third time.

"I'm lost."

Cinders stretched her neck over Mary Jane's shoulder and looked down. "Go left."

They flew along the highway for several miles. The ground looked familiar now. There was Ocean Parkway.

Mary Jane sighed with relief. She pointed the wand homeward. Marian clutched the hose desperately. Any minute she might fall and crash onto the roof of a car. Her wet jeans stuck to her skin. She wasn't at all sure she liked magic.

In the joy of steering the vacuum cleaner Mary Jane forgot her wet clothes.

When at last she flew past the park and the school and over the apartment building down to her own window, she was quite an expert. She steered James in the window and landed softly in the middle of the floor.

Marian untangled herself from the hose and looked around in a dazed way.

Mrs. Brooks came to the door. "You're back! I was beginning to worry. Why didn't you let me know when you came in?" When she saw the wet clothes all she said was, "I don't think you ever go near that lake in Prospect Park without falling in." She looked around at the untidy room. "I see you didn't get very far with that vacuum cleaner. I'll have to show you how to use it."

MORE MISCHIEF

Cinders was such a nuisance in school on Monday and Tuesday that Mary Jane refused to take her on Wednesday. Coming home alone in the afternoon, Mary Jane had just reached the block where she lived when she looked up and saw Hilda. The witch came flying on roller skates over the apartment building on the corner.

Hilda held her arms out on either side to balance herself and took long glides in the air. The witch was having fun. She chased a pair of sparrows and skimmed over a rooftop. When she reached Mary Jane's house, she swooped down and landed on the front walk.

Mary Jane watched Hilda take off the

skates, fold them as small as a handkerchief, and tuck them in her apron pocket.

The witch clumped up the front walk,
her feet heavy and slow without the skates.
Mary Jane ran up behind her and tapped
her on the shoulder. Hilda spun around.
"What do you want?"

"What do *you* want?" asked Mary Jane.

"My vacuum cleaner, of course."

"Then give back my skates."

"I can't give you the skates now. I did
a lot of work on them," cried the witch
angrily, "and you'd better give me my
vacuum cleaner!"

"What will you do if I don't?"

"Wait and see." The witch felt in her
pocket for the magic scissors.

Mary Jane slipped her quick little hand
under Hilda's big clumsy one and pulled
the scissors out of the pocket. With a snip
she brought Hilda down to her own size,

and then, snip, snip, snip—the witch was only three and a half inches tall. Mary Jane held her in one hand.

"Stop, stop!" screamed the witch.

Mary Jane stopped. "Oh, dear! I *am* sorry. I never meant to do *this* to you."

Hilda glared. "The way you were going," she moaned, "I would soon have disappeared completely."

"You reached for the scissors first," reminded Mary Jane.

"That has nothing to do with it," sulked the witch. "Now I can't get home. The skates have shrunk too. It would take an age to go ten blocks."

"I never thought of that." Mary Jane looked at the witch standing on the palm of her hand, tiny hands on her hips, feet spread apart. "You know," she mused, "you're just the right size for my doll-house, and I don't have any dolls. I wonder if Cinders would mind."

Mary Jane popped Hilda into her lunch box and rang the doorbell. Her mother opened the door and greeted her with a hug. After a quick hug in return Mary Jane slipped away upstairs. From the dollhouse Cinders called, "Did you bring me some food?"

"I left a piece of sausage in my lunch box. And, oh, Cinders, could the witch share the dollhouse with you? There's plenty of room, and she has nowhere to live."

Cinders looked suspiciously at Mary Jane. "What have you been up to?"

Mary Jane opened the lunch box. The witch had fainted. "Cinders," she cried, "what's wrong with her?"

"Probably the smell of sausage. And, by the way, you forgot to give it to me."

Mary Jane gently laid the witch in the pink and white guest bed of the dollhouse. She threw Cinders the sausage and ran to get some water to bathe the witch's forehead. Hilda slowly opened her eyes and looked around the dainty doll's bedroom. She saw Mary Jane's enormous face looking in. "Drat!" said the witch.

"Would you like something to eat?" asked Mary Jane politely.

"I'm sure you have no witch's brew," said Hilda sadly.

Only last night Mary Jane had tried mixing toothpaste with some of her mother's perfume. She had put it in a baby aspirin bottle which still had a few crumbs left. After breakfast she added some orange juice. Now she took the bottle out of her desk drawer, shook it, and filled a tiny cup. She put the cup on the doll's dining room table.

Hilda sat up in bed, her sharp nose quivering. She pattered down the little stairway and trotted into the dining room. Hardly daring to believe her nose, she approached the table. "It smells like something I haven't had since I was a child. What is it?"

"Just a little pretend witch's brew," said Mary Jane. "I didn't really like it, but you might."

Hilda lifted the cup and sniffed it with delight. "Smells delicious," she said, and took a sip. "M-m-m-m. It *is* delicious!"

The witch sat on a little chair and drank the whole cupful. Then she had a second helping. Mary Jane felt very proud.

After drinking her second cupful, Hilda walked into the kitchen, where she found Cinders holding both paws over her nose. "How did you get here? I put you in my pocket."

"I fell out."

Hilda took another look. "Are you sure you're my cat? You sound like her, but you don't look like her. I couldn't put up with *you*." She frowned and shook a finger at

Cinders. "Do you know that you are positively fat! No witch's cat is ever fat."

Hilda looked around. "I'll have to make this house more home-like if I'm to be living here." She took down the curtains and stuffed them under the sofa, scattered the pots and pans and dishes around the kitchen and dining room, and changed the chairs from one room to another. She managed to carry a heavy living room chair upstairs and place it in the bathtub. She piled the rugs on top of one of the beds and moved the little books Mary Jane and Marian had made to the kitchen sink. At last Hilda dusted her hands. "There now," she said, "that looks better."

Mary Jane had gone to see Marian to tell her the news. Marian was weeding her garden. She went on weeding while Mary Jane told of the latest doings of the witch.

Marian raised her head. "I guess now we never will play with the dollhouse. I saw just the right dolls in Woolworth's yesterday. You can dress and undress them too."

"But, Marian," said Mary Jane, "it's more fun to have a real live witch living in the dollhouse. I don't suppose, though, that she'll let us dress and undress her."

Mary Jane helped her friend with the weeding. Marian had just time before supper to run over and look at the witch. Mrs. Brooks met them at the door. "Mary Jane, I don't like to scold, but I told you to take care of that dollhouse. Aunt Harriet went to a lot of trouble to send it. I went upstairs to put your laundry away and I saw that the dollhouse is a frightful mess. If you can't keep it neat we'll put it away until you're older."

Mary Jane and Marian raced up to Mary Jane's room. The dollhouse was a

shambles. Mary Jane looked through the
dollhouse as she set it to rights. She found
Cinders behind the clock.

"Where is the witch?" Mary Jane was
frantic.

"Oh," said Cinders glumly, "she flew
away on those old roller skates."

The window was closed. Mary Jane
and Marian went to Mrs. Brooks's room.

They heard a little clicking from the dresser. Hilda had managed to pull the stopper out of the perfume and had got her head stuck in the bottle. Her legs were waving in the air with the roller skates still on her feet.

Marian grabbed the bottle, and Mary Jane held the witch. By turning her like a stopper they pulled her out.

Hilda stood on the roller skates on the dresser and smoothed her skirt. She picked up her hat and put it back on her head. She looked a bit shamefaced. "I thought it was bigger than it was." Seeing Marian, she asked, "Who is that?"

"This is my friend, Marian. Marian, this is the famous Witch Hilda."

Hilda looked pleased. She was not a powerful or important witch, and it was nice to have someone call her famous. She bowed to Marian, who said, "How do you do?"

Marian had to go home for supper. Mary Jane went back to straighten the dollhouse, and Hilda continued to explore Mrs. Brooks's dressing table. The cold-cream lid was loose. Hilda accidentally sat in it. She skated to the bedspread and rolled in it to get the cold cream off. Then she tied the venetian-blind cords together to make a flying trapeze and used a pink lipstick to draw a lovely picture on the wall.

Wanting someone to admire her drawing, Hilda went to look for Mary Jane. She almost skated into Mr. Brooks's face as she flew down the hall. With a sharp left turn she whizzed past his ear.

"Somebody left a window open. There's a bat in here!" called Mary Jane's father.

Mary Jane came running. She had never had a close look at a bat.

Hilda was insulted. "Bat indeed!" she said, and decided to go home to the dollhouse. She skated into the upstairs bathroom. "I know I put a chair in that tub," said Hilda. She skated through the whole house. All her work had been undone. The house was just as neat and unfriendly as before.

"Drat!" said the witch. She was close to tears, but she bravely started all over again to put the dollhouse in comfortable disorder.

Mary Jane and her father had not been able to find the bat so they went downstairs to supper. Mary Jane stored a piece of chicken in her pocket for Cinders, but she didn't know what to feed the witch.

After supper Mary Jane wanted Cinders to help with her homework. When she looked in the dollhouse for the cat, she found the house a complete mess again. Hilda was wearily pushing an easy chair up the stairs. She had taken off the skates and put them back in her pocket.

"Why, Witch Hilda, what are you

doing?" gasped Mary Jane. "I just finished straightening that house."

Hilda sat down on the stairs and let go
of the chair. Mary Jane caught it before it
could fall. She put it back in the living
room.

"I think," said Hilda bitterly, "that we
have to get a few things straight around
here—and I don't mean this house. If I'm
to live in it, I ought to be allowed to make
it comfortable. I am not comfortable in
straight houses."

"But, Witch Hilda," said Mary Jane,
"my mother will take the
dollhouse away if I
don't keep it neat."

"I want to
go home."

At this
moment Mary
Jane's father
came into the

room. Hilda hid in a corner of the doll-house stairway.

Mr. Brooks took one look at the doll-house. He held Mary Jane's arm and led her down the hall to show her the drawing on the wall, the cold cream on the bed-spread, and the tangle of cords by the window.

Mary Jane tried to tell her father it was the witch who had made the mess, but he did not believe her.

"Now," said Mr. Brooks, "go clean up your room."

Mary Jane went back to her room to find the witch once more trying to drag the easy chair up the stairs.

"Come on," sobbed Mary Jane, "I'll take you home."

She pulled out the vacuum cleaner and found Cinders behind the doll-house clock. Luckily Mary Jane was wearing a dress with two pockets. She put

Cinders in one and the witch in the other.

"Don't forget food!" cried the cat. Mary Jane went quietly down to the kitchen and loaded a shopping bag with a container of milk, two apples, half a loaf of bread, and a jar of peanut butter. "Tuna fish," begged Cinders. Mary Jane packed two small cans and a can opener.

Back upstairs she mounted the vacuum cleaner, wound the hose around her neck, and pointed the wand toward the open window. "Witch Town, James."

Shakily James rose into the air. He felt sick because Mary Jane's mother had used him to clean the basement playroom, and the dust was still in him. With a cough he cleared the windowsill and sailed out into the summer night.

THE WITCH'S IDEA

Sometimes Cinders told Mary Jane where to point the wand, and other times the witch gave directions. James was very slow.

"I think," said Cinders, "that he'd fly faster if you emptied the dust out of him."

Mary Jane brought the vacuum cleaner down on top of an office building. She climbed off, opened the clasps on the jug, and carefully shook out the dust.

After that James went more quickly. He seemed to remember the way himself. Faster and faster, over forests and lakes. He crossed wide oceans and strange dark valleys. The fires of Witch Town blazed below. James flew into the open mouth of Witch Hilda's cave. Mary Jane tumbled off the vacuum cleaner. She was tired from the trip, but Hilda had strapped on the roller skates and came flying out of her pocket.

The witch was in high spirits. "I have an idea! I have an idea!" she chanted. "Mary Jane, help me."

Hilda's excitement was catching. Mary Jane jumped to her feet. "What can I do?"

Hilda flew to her battered old recipe book. "Look up measuring tape."

"How do you spell it?"

"M-E-G-H-E . . . ," began Hilda.

Cinders meowed loudly. Mary Jane lifted her out of her pocket and placed her on her shoulder. "I may be fat," said Cinders to the witch, "but I can still spell— M-E-A-S-U-R-I-N-G T-A-P-E."

Mary Jane leafed through the book. Hilda stuck a torch in a crack in the wall. By its flickering light Mary Jane made out the words. "Magnet," she read, "mailbox, match, measles. Oh here it is. Measuring tape."

Hilda was bobbing about in the air in wild excitement. "What do we need, Mary Jane?"

"For a magic measuring tape start with twenty pieces of cooked macaroni taken from the plate of a hungry man. Sew these together with twenty white hairs of an old woman. Put the attached

97

macaroni in a pot of thick witch's brew with four rattlesnake rattles. Dance the can-can around the pot for four minutes, and then recite the Gettysburg Address."

"That's an easy one," said the witch. "Could you copy it down? We'll have to go back to the World of Human Beings for those things. Nobody in Witch Town eats macaroni. By the way, I'm hungry. Could I interest you in a nice hot cup of witch's brew?"

Mary Jane looked toward the huge pot bubbling away in the corner of the cave. The smell from it was hard to believe. "No, thank you. I'm not hungry."

"But I am," meowed Cinders. "You forgot to give me supper."

Mary Jane felt in the pocket where the witch had been. She found the bit of chicken. It was almost as good as when she had put it there. Mary Jane gave it to the cat.

Hilda meantime was having trouble getting anything to eat. The spoon was too big for her to lift, and she was afraid to stand on the rim of the pot with her skates on. Once more she had to ask Mary Jane for help.

Mary Jane scooped up a spoonful of brew, and Hilda skated out of the cave and came back with an acorn cup. Mary Jane filled the cup twice before the witch was satisfied.

"Now," said Hilda, when she had finished her second helping, "are you up to flying home again?"

"She had better rest first," said Cinders.

Mary Jane was indeed tired from her long trip. There was a pile of feathers on the floor of the cave. She covered them with a cloak of Hilda's and lay down. In no time she was fast asleep, with the little cat curled against her neck.

THE WITCH IN SCHOOL

When Mary Jane awoke it was broad day-light. "Oh," she cried, "it's Thursday morning. I must get to school. I wonder what time it is."

Cinders yawned and stretched. "It's early, silly. Have you forgotten that it's June?" The cat cocked an eye at the sun. "My guess is that it's about five o'clock in the morning. Let's have breakfast and see how fast James can get you home."

Both Mary Jane and Cinders had milk, and Mary Jane ate an apple and a peanut butter sandwich as well. Hilda was asleep in the bowl of her big spoon, the roller skates still on her feet. Mary Jane gently put her in her pocket. She filled a

bottle with witch's brew and climbed on the vacuum cleaner.

Yesterday's journey had put James back in practice. In almost no time at all Mary Jane flew into the open window of her bedroom. She climbed off the vacuum cleaner and shoved it into the closet. Peeking in the mirror she saw that her face was dirty and her hair tangled, but there was still time for a shower.

Mary Jane changed into fresh clothes, taking care to choose a dress with two pockets. She sat at her desk to do her homework. Cinders helped with the spelling.

She was nearly finished when her mother came in. "I see you never straightened your room, Mary Jane. It's time I had a talk with you, but we'd better wait till after school. It took hours to clean up my room last night. I never even got around to say good night to you. I wonder why your father gave me a perfume named 'Mischief.' There's quite enough of that around here already. Now hurry or you'll be late for school."

Mary Jane picked up her books. She put the bottle of witch's brew in her lunch box along with a doll's cup and went downstairs for her sandwiches.

The witch and the cat rode to school in Mary Jane's pockets. Hilda gave no trouble. She went to sleep almost at once, but Cinders had the hiccups. She made so much noise that Mary Jane had to pretend she had them. Mrs. Carson nearly discovered the cat when Mary Jane gave Cinders a drink at the drinking fountain.

All morning Mary Jane tried not to attract attention. To her relief the cat finally fell asleep. Hilda was snoring in one pocket and Cinders in the other, but luckily only Mary Jane could hear the snores.

She met Marian for lunch. By then both the witch and the cat were hungry. Mary Jane put them in the lunch box with a cup of cold witch's brew and a bit of meat from her sandwich. Then she told Marian about last night's events. "Now," she finished, "where do I get the macaroni?"

"Easy," said Marian. "Buy some and get your mother to cook it for your father."

"How can I make my mother cook it?"

"Tell her you want it for supper."

"She knows I don't like it."

"Does your father like it?"

"If it has cheese on it."

Witch Hilda could bear it no longer. "Please," she piped in her tiny voice, "change the subject. You are making me ill."

In the afternoon Mrs. Carson gave a science lesson. It was so interesting that Hilda poked her head out to listen. At sight of the teacher the witch stiffened all over. Her green eyes stared at Mrs. Carson's pretty white hair. Before Mary Jane could stop her she climbed out of her pocket. The roller skates were on her feet. When Mrs. Carson bent her head over a magnet she wanted to show the class, Hilda skated through the air to the blackboard behind the teacher's desk. Several children saw her. She looked like a black beetle sitting on the ledge for the chalk.

"What's that at the blackboard?" asked a boy. Mrs. Carson turned to look, and the witch skated onto her head.

"There's a bug on you, Mrs. Carson!" screamed one of the girls.

Mrs. Carson felt something pull her hair. She slapped at it, but Hilda was too quick for her. She yanked out three shining hairs and skated off to hide in the coat closet.

By now the children were running up and down the aisles and yelling. Mrs. Carson rapped with a ruler on her desk.

"Quiet!" she commanded. She opened her handbag and took out a mirror and comb to straighten her hair. A few white hairs were caught in the teeth of the comb. The teacher neatly pulled them off and tossed them into her wastebasket.

"Cinders," whispered Mary Jane, "did you see that?"

"Put me on the floor," said Cinders. Mary Jane pretended to pick up an eraser and set the little cat on the floor.

Cinders carefully picked her way through the children's feet. Going quietly on her soft paws she reached the wastebasket. It was made of wire and she crawled right into it. With a little rustling of paper she pulled the white hairs out of the basket.

At this point Hilda skated out of the coat closet straight at Mrs. Carson's head. The teacher waved her arms wildly, but Hilda was like a dive bomber circling up and zooming down to snatch a hair or two each time.

Again the children were on their feet.

Mary Jane was afraid Cinders would be trampled in the excitement. She slipped over to the wastebasket and rescued the little cat. Cinders proudly showed her four white hairs neatly wound around her paw.

With Cinders safe in her pocket Mary Jane went to help the witch. Two of the boys were trying to catch her. Hilda darted here and there playing tag. Now and then she snatched another hair from the poor teacher's head.

"I think I can catch it," said Mary Jane. "Hold still, Mrs. Carson. If it lands on your head I'll grab it."

Hilda understood. The boys drew

back to give Mary Jane room. Hilda landed neatly on the teacher's head and began to pluck hairs as if she were pulling the petals off a daisy. Mary Jane cupped her hands over the witch and then went swiftly to the window and threw her out. Hilda skated off toward Mary Jane's house.

"Thank you, Mary Jane," said Mrs. Carson. "Now, children, let's get back to our science lesson. Who here has made an electromagnet?"

MACARONI MAGIC

At three o'clock Mary Jane and Marian walked home together. When Mary Jane reached her front door she waved goodbye to her friend. Her mother was waiting for her at the door.

"It's time for our talk, Mary Jane. Come in the kitchen and have some milk."

Cinders was in Mary Jane's pocket. At the mention of milk she began to stir around. Mary Jane filled a bottle cap with milk from her glass and cupped her hand over the cat while she drank. Mrs. Brooks was busy at the sink and didn't notice. Mary Jane seldom had trouble hiding things from her. She wasn't like Mrs. Carson, who noticed everything.

"Mary Jane, it's time you started to

grow up. I don't understand how a big girl like you could act like a four-year-old. Daddy is very angry."

"Mother, let's fix a special treat for Daddy. Make macaroni and cheese for supper."

"You know you don't like it."

"But Daddy likes it. I'll have tuna fish."

"That reminds me. Mary Jane, what are those cans of tuna fish doing in the shopping bag in your room? Were you planning to run away from home?"

Mary Jane did not answer. She peeked under her hand to make sure Cinders had finished her milk. She put the cat back in her pocket.

"Please, Mother, let me cook the macaroni for Daddy."

"Then you will have to run to the store for it. I don't have any in the house."

Before going to the store, Mary Jane

changed into play clothes. She looked into the dollhouse and found Hilda counting the white hairs as she lined them up on a bed. "Seventeen," said the witch.

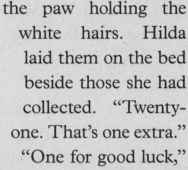

Cinders meowed and held up the paw holding the white hairs. Hilda laid them on the bed beside those she had collected. "Twenty-one. That's one extra."

"One for good luck," said Cinders. She scampered around chasing her tail. Cinders was pleased with herself.

After Mary Jane returned from the store, she put a pan of water to boil on the kitchen stove. Her mother helped her with the cheese sauce.

When Mr. Brooks came home he walked into the kitchen to find a snack. Mary Jane was waiting for him. "Please wait for supper, Daddy. I want you to be really hungry."

"I'll be hungry," her father promised, taking a box of crackers out of the cabinet.

At this moment Hilda skated into the room and circled Mr. Brooks's head. He was so startled that he dropped the crackers. "It's that bat again!" he exclaimed.

Quietly Mary Jane picked up the crackers and hid them.

By supper time Mr. Brooks was very hungry. He sat at the table, and Mary Jane's mother served him a plateful of macaroni and cheese. As he was about to take a bite, Mary Jane let out a yell. "Watch out! There's that bat again." She jumped out of her chair, ran around the table, and knocked her father's plate to the floor. It smashed into a dozen pieces.

"I'm sorry," said Mary Jane. "I'll clean up the mess."

Her mother and father looked at her as if she were crazy. Mrs. Brooks spooned out another serving of macaroni on a fresh plate while Mary Jane picked up the broken one.

She put the spilled macaroni in a basin. At the kitchen sink she washed the sauce off twenty pieces and stored them in a plastic bag. She stuffed the bag in her pocket and went back to the dining room table. Her mother and father had decided it was best to ignore the strange way Mary Jane was acting. They ate supper as if nothing had happened.

After she had helped her mother with the dishes, Mary Jane found a needle in her mother's sewing box and took it to her room.

Cinders was in the kitchen of the dollhouse hoping for some tuna fish. Mary Jane ran back downstairs to get the tuna-fish can before her mother threw it out.

Her father met her walking upstairs with the can.

"What's that for?" he asked.

"Cinders."

"I thought we didn't have that cat anymore," said Mr. Brooks. Mary Jane went quickly to her room. She put Cinders right into the can.

"I'll have a terrible time getting myself clean after this," grumbled Cinders.

"I'm afraid you won't get enough to eat any other way," explained Mary Jane. Cinders began licking the can clean while Mary Jane took the macaroni out of her pocket. Hilda came flying out of the dollhouse on the roller skates. "Put it on the floor end to end," she said.

With some help from Hilda, Mary Jane threaded the needle with a white hair. She sewed the pieces of macaroni together, making a long chain. Mary Jane coiled the macaroni inside the empty tuna-fish can and made a lid with a rubber band and a handkerchief.

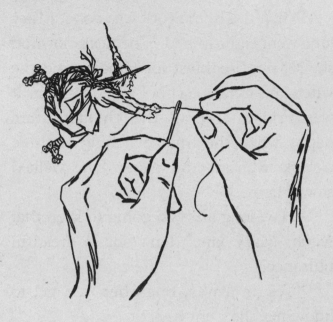

"I'll do my homework now, and then we'd all better go to sleep. Tomorrow we'll figure out how to get the rattlesnake rattles."

"They're no problem," said Hilda. "Everybody has them in Witch Town. I may even have a few in my cave, back in the corner with the octopus ink and turtles' teeth."

When the homework was done, Mary Jane went right to bed. The next morning she set out breakfast for Cinders and the witch and went to school without them. It was Friday, and all the children were happy when the final bell rang at three o'clock. Marian and Mary Jane walked slowly home.

"How long are you going to keep that witch, Mary Jane? Isn't she a dreadful nuisance?"

"Yes, in a way, but when you get to know her she's not bad."

"I don't trust her," said Marian. "What happened to those scissors?"

"I put them in a safe place. You never know when they'll come in handy."

When they reached Mary Jane's house, Marian decided to come in for a while. Mrs. Brooks opened the door and went back to the telephone. She was talking excitedly to someone.

Upstairs the two girls found Hilda surrounded by all the parts of a tiny vacuum cleaner. "Hilda," Mary Jane cried, "what are you doing to my mother's vacuum cleaner? First you snipped it small. Now you're taking it apart."

"Mary Jane, I could fix this if I had the right size screwdriver."

"I still have the magic scissors," said Mary Jane. "I could snip a screwdriver down to size, but what if Daddy needed it?"

"Mary Jane," said Hilda, "you have to take that chance."

In the end Mary Jane snipped down quite a few tools and nuts and bolts and washers from her father's workbench. Hilda worked on the vacuum cleaner for nearly an hour while Cinders kept track of all the parts.

Mary Jane and Marian went to the hardware store for batteries for the dollhouse. Now they could plug the vacuum cleaner into the little wall outlets.

Hilda enjoyed her work. She said it was a lot like magic and not nearly so dangerous. The witch was pleased and proud when all the parts were back in place, and the tiny vacuum cleaner worked like a charm. She did refuse to clean the dollhouse, though. Marian vacuumed it from top to bottom. "If I thought I'd be living here much longer I'd never allow it," said Hilda. She flew about Mary Jane's bedroom on the roller skates so as not to be in Marian's way.

When Mary Jane heard her mother call she ran downstairs. "Mary Jane," said Mrs. Brooks, "some old friends telephoned. They want Daddy and me to meet them for dinner and go to a play. I can't get a sitter for you. Could you cook your own supper? I'll put a TV dinner in the oven. All you have to do is turn it on for a few minutes."

"I don't need a baby-sitter, and of course I can get my own supper. When are you leaving?"

"As soon as I can."

After Marian had gone home Mary Jane watched her mother dress. Mrs. Brooks powdered her nose and put on some of her new perfume called "Mischief." As soon as the stopper was off the bottle Mary Jane ran to her own room and grabbed Hilda. The witch was getting ready to skate after the wonderful smell. Mary Jane could hardly hang on to her. Finally she locked her in her desk drawer and went back to say good-bye to her mother. Then she returned to let Hilda out of her prison.

"Don't be angry, Witch Hilda," she said. "If my mother saw you it would spoil everything. She'd take an aspirin and lie down. Then, how would I get away? Hurry now, let's get back to Witch Town."

The thought of working on her magic spell cheered Hilda. Mary Jane stuffed her in a pocket with Cinders. The tuna-fish can with the macaroni in it went into the other pocket. Soon they were on their way.

They flew along at a remarkable speed. In almost no time the vacuum cleaner arrived at the witch's cave.

The fire was out under the big iron pot. Mary Jane made a few trips on the vacuum cleaner to the forest at the foot of the mountain to get firewood. Hilda took her last match to re-light the fire.

When the brew was once more bubbling and steaming, Mary Jane read the

recipe again. Suddenly the witch stopped
skating and came to rest on the shelf near
her big book. "Drat!" said Hilda. "It isn't
Wednesday!"

"What's so special about Wednesday?"

Hilda drew herself up to her full three and a half inches. "I was *born* on a Wednesday, and that's really the only day I can be certain a spell will work."

"Isn't there anything we can do?" asked Mary Jane sadly.

A gleam of hope flickered in Hilda's green eyes. "Mary Jane," she asked hoarsely, "do you know what day *you* were born on?"

Mary Jane knew very well. Her mother often told her, "Friday's child is loving and giving."

"Friday," she told the witch.

Hilda sprang into action. "Hurry, Mary Jane, perhaps we still have time. I don't think it's midnight yet. If *you* throw the things into the pot perhaps the spell will work. That pretend witch's brew of yours was very good."

With trembling hands Mary Jane

found the four rattlesnake rattles, but then she gasped, "Oh, dear!"

"What's the matter?" asked Hilda, who was skating in little circles around the pot. "I don't know how to do the can-can!"

Hilda laughed and held up her skirt. Still on roller skates she started to dance the can-can. Her pointed hat bobbed up and down.

Mary Jane threw the macaroni and the rattlesnake rattles into the boiling brew. The witch danced round and round on her roller skates.

Only one more thing was needed to cast the spell. "Hilda," asked Mary Jane, "do you know the Gettysburg Address?"

"No." Hilda continued to dance.

"Neither do I." Mary Jane felt like crying. All their work was for nothing!

And then, out of the darkness of the cave, a small voice came. "Four score and seven years ago—" it began.

Cinders was reciting the Gettysburg Address.

Magic Measure

Mary Jane was very quiet. From the old iron pot a pale green steam rose in hissing spurts. The boiling liquid rose higher and higher and finally bubbled over the edge of the pot and streamed down onto the fire below. With a crackling sputter like a machine gun, the fire went out.

With the big spoon Mary Jane fished down in the thick slimy depths of the pot. She scooped up the first thing the spoon touched. It was a tape measure, white and bright, neatly coiled into a spool, and very, very long! Mary Jane lifted it off the spoon and walked to the mouth of the cave to examine it in the starlight.

"Light a torch," squeaked Hilda. "Aren't there any more matches?"

"No."

"Well, maybe we can work it in the dark. I'll stand on one end of the tape measure."

Hilda had taken off the skates and was perched on the edge of the shelf. Mary Jane took her down and planted her on one end of the tape measure. The witch stood as tall as she could. "Measure me."

As Mary Jane unrolled the tape, the witch became taller and taller. At last Mary Jane stood on her tiptoes with her hands above her head. The witch towered black above her.

"There," said Hilda in her harsh loud voice, "this seems to be the right size." She stepped off the tape measure, and it coiled back into the spool in Mary Jane's hand with a snap.

The witch fixed her green eyes on Mary Jane. "How you've shrunk," she said. "Now, let's see about that cat." She grabbed the tape measure and looked around for Cinders. Holding her by the nape of her neck she measured her.

When Cinders wriggled free and darted to a far corner of the cave, she was a regular-sized cat.

"I think you made her a little bigger than she used to be," Mary Jane said.

She looked around. It was very dark. Mary Jane had forgotten how frightening the witch was when she was her usual size. "I think I'd better go home."

"Can you get home alone, Mary Jane?"

"I—I don't know."

"Hey, you!" Hilda screeched. Cinders crept trembling from the shadows. "You're not really a bad cat, but you're much too fat. All of Witch Town would laugh at me if I kept a cat like you. I'm afraid you'll have to go. Perhaps Mary Jane will let you live with her. At any rate, I want you to guide her home."

Mary Jane seated herself on the vacuum cleaner, and Cinders rode on the hose as it stretched out behind like a snake. "My house, James."

The trip home didn't take long. Several times Cinders had to tell Mary Jane the way but they reached Mary Jane's window in good time.

As soon as she had put James in the closet, Mary Jane ran down to the kitchen. She was hungry. She looked in the oven. The TV dinner was warm but rather dried up by now. Mary Jane shared it with the cat. Then she went to sleep with Cinders curled up on the foot of her bed.

In the morning, when Mary Jane's mother came to wake her, she found the cat in her room. She bent down and scratched her behind the ears. Cinders arched her back and purred. She rubbed against Mrs. Brooks's leg.

"Cinders," said Mrs. Brooks, "wherever did you come from?"

The cat just purred louder. Mrs. Brooks picked her up and held her against her cheek. "Come down to the kitchen and have some breakfast. Mary Jane, wake up! How did Cinders get in your room?"

"Through the window," answered Mary Jane.

"She must have run away from that woman," reasoned her mother. "If she comes for her I'm afraid we'll have to give Cinders back." She pursed her lips and added grimly, "She'll have to take her vacuum cleaner back too. I don't like the way it works at all. I could do better with a broom. By the way, Mary Jane, what did you do with Daddy's tools? He's been looking everywhere for them."

The doorbell rang, and Mrs. Brooks went to see who was there. It was Marian, who had come to play with Mary Jane as she did every Saturday.

Mary Jane rushed to dress and eat breakfast. As soon as Marian saw Cinders, she said, "I see your macaroni worked. Did you get rid of that old witch? I want to play with the dollhouse."

"Wouldn't you like to take a trip on the vacuum cleaner? We could go to the zoo."

"I told my mother I'd be at your house."

Cinders was busy helping Mrs. Brooks with the dusting. Mary Jane and Marian decided to re-arrange the furniture in the dollhouse. Marian wanted to make kitchen curtains, with Kleenex and Scotch tape. While the two girls were working, they heard a tap on the window. They looked up to see Hilda peeking in.

Mary Jane opened the window. At sight of the full-sized witch Marian drew back in terror. Even Mary Jane felt a little afraid.

Skating into the room, Hilda said breathlessly, "Quick, Mary Jane, give me the little vacuum cleaner and the tools."

Mary Jane pulled them out of her desk drawer. With the measuring tape Hilda carefully returned each one to its proper size.

"Put the tools back on your father's bench," said the witch. "I'll take your mother's vacuum cleaner."

It was quite a trick for Hilda to hold the vacuum cleaner in mid-air and skate out the window with it, but she managed it. She flew around to the front of the house, took off the skates, and tucked them in her pocket. With the vacuum cleaner in hand she marched up the front steps and pressed the bell. Mary Jane's mother opened the door. Her eyes opened wide when she saw the witch.

"Good day, Madam," said Hilda politely. "I came to return your vacuum cleaner. It's in perfect condition now. I'd like to have the other one back now, if you please."

"Yes, certainly," said Mrs. Brooks. Sadly she added, "I suppose you'll want your cat back too. You know she came back to us. Please won't you let me buy her from you?"

Hilda blinked her green eyes. "You mean you *want* that fat cat?"

"I do."

"Well, then, by all means keep her. Only do let me have my vacuum cleaner."

"Just a minute." Mrs. Brooks went upstairs to Mary Jane's room. "You'll never guess who is at the front door," she said. "It's that funny little fat woman.

She's brought back our old vacuum cleaner. And oh, Mary Jane, she said we can keep Cinders! Now, take her old vacuum cleaner down to her—it isn't good for much."

Mary Jane carried James downstairs to the front door. She gave him to the witch. "Hilda," she whispered, "promise you won't kick him anymore."

Hilda looked down at Mary Jane. Suddenly she smiled. She reached into her apron pocket and pulled out a flat packet. With a little shake she unfolded it into a pair of roller skates—the magic folding flying skates.

"They're yours, Mary Jane," she said, and handed them to her. Then the witch seated herself on the vacuum cleaner. She looped the hose around her neck, raised the wand, and sang out, "Home, James!"

The vacuum cleaner rose slowly into

the air and sailed higher and higher, up over the treetops, higher than the apartment building on the corner. At last it sailed away out of sight.

LET THE MAGIC CONTINUE. . . .

Here's a sneak peek
at another tale
by Ruth Chew!

WITCH'S BROOM

Amy straddled the broomstick. "Come on, Blue Boy, let's go for a ride."

The broom seemed to quiver. Suddenly it began to jog around the kitchen. The blue bristles dragged on the floor. So did Amy's feet.

"Ow!" Amy's ankle banged against one of the kitchen chairs. She held tight to the broomstick and tried to yank it upright. "Up, Blue Boy, up!"

Without any warning the broom zoomed up into the air. Amy ducked her head just in time to keep it from crashing into the ceiling. "Steady, Blue Boy, steady!"

The broom bounced up and down. It seemed to be trying to throw Amy to the ground. She wrapped her legs around the stick and hung on with both hands. "Easy, Boy, easy!"

Jean started to laugh. "You look like a cowboy on a bucking bronco."

"Maybe you think you can do better," Amy snapped.

At this the broom glided to the floor. Amy got off. She handed the broom to Jean. "Your turn."

Jean stroked the broom handle. "Nice Blue Boy," she said. She patted the blue bristles. Then she sat down on the bristles and waited. The broom lay quiet on the floor. "Please, Magic Broom," Jean said, "won't you take me for a ride?"

Still the broom lay on the floor.

All at once Amy had an idea. "Maybe it's a *girl*!"

Jean stood up. She turned the broom over and held it with the bristles up. "What a pretty broom it is! Of course it's a girl."

Very slowly the broom swayed back and forth.

"Look, Jean," Amy said. "She's trying to nod. And I think she likes to have her bristles up."

Again the little broom nodded.

"No wonder she was angry with me," Amy said. "I was holding her upside-down!"